RALPH'S

ELISE · PRIMAVERA

The Putnam & Grosset Book Group, 200 Madison Avenue, New York, NY 10016. Published simultaneously in Canada.
Printed in Hong Kong by South China Printing Co. (1988) Ltd. Book design by Nanette Stevenson. Lettering by David Gatti.
Library of Congress Cataloging-in-Publication Data Primavera, Elise. Ralph's frozen tale / Elise Primavera. p. cm. Summary: Ralph,
a fearless explorer on his way to the North Pole, meets a friendly polar bear who helps him in his journey. 1. Explorers—Fiction. 2. Polar bear—
Fiction. 3. Bears—Fiction. 4. North Pole—Fiction] I. Title. PZ7.P935 Ral 1991 [E]—dc20 90-35521 CIP AC ISBN 0-399-22252-9
1 3 5 7 9 10 8 6 4 2

First impression

#21562928

FROZEN TALE

G.P. PUTNAM'S SONS · NEW YORK

Ralph was an explorer. He loved the excitement and the danger. Once he even went over the treacherous Ungabangi Falls alone in a kayak, laughing out loud all the way to the bottom.

People were always yelling "Hooray for Ralph!" and telling him how brave he was.

But Ralph wasn't happy. "What's left for me to do?" he said one day as he stood signing autographs. "I've been everywhere."

KABAM! An icicle cracked off and bopped him on the head. "That's it," he shouted. "I'm going to the North Pole!"

So he packed his mukluks and his muffler and his woolly mittens. He bought a couple of huskies, a sled, and a book on dogsledding. And off he went.

Ralph and his huskies made their way farther and farther north. "This is going to be easy," he said as they passed the last town, the last tree, the last bird.

"HA HA! I laugh at danger," he shouted out. "There's nothing left but me, my huskies, and my dog-sled!"

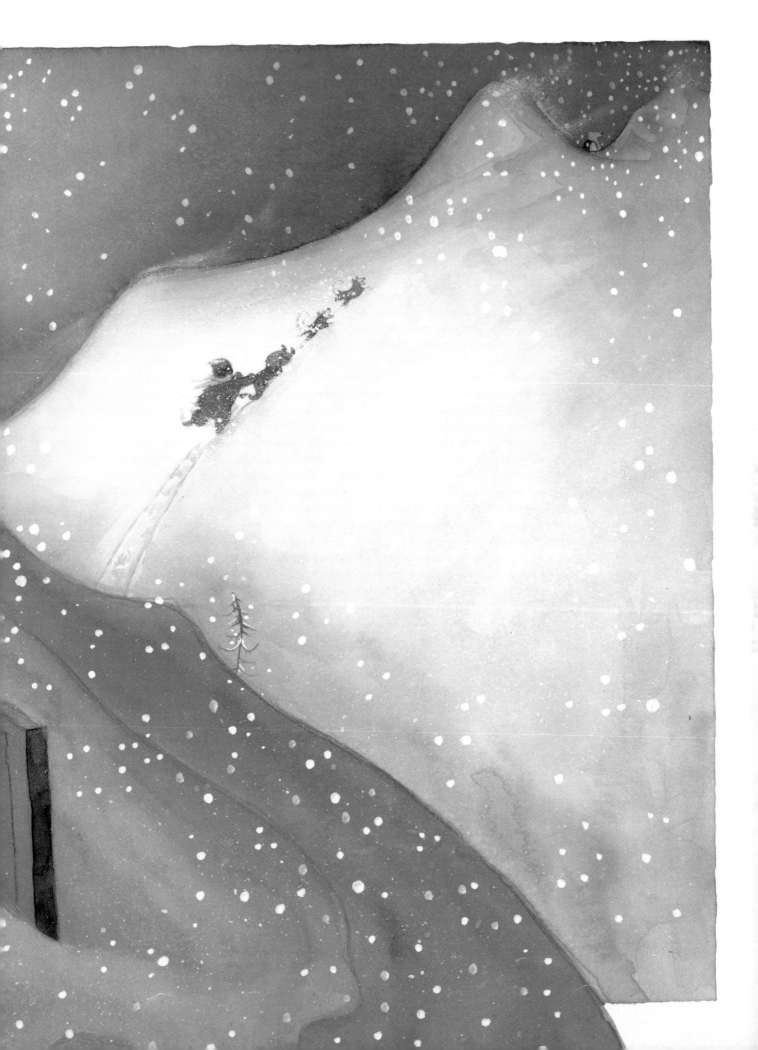

That night Ralph was awakened by a bloodcurdling howl. His huskies got very excited and peeked out of the tent. When they saw wolves, they ran off in hot pursuit.

"HA HA!" Ralph said as he watched his dogs disappear over the horizon. "I laugh at being alone in the middle of nowhere with no dogs!"

Without his huskies the going was tougher. His mukluks were killing him as he struggled through the wind and snow. All of a sudden his dogsled disappeared in front of him. He looked down into the yawning mouth of a giant crevasse and heard his words echo back at him. ''HA HA! I laugh at danger. I laugh at being alone in the middle of nowhere with no dogs and no dogsled.''

All that laughing soon made Ralph
hungry. But before you could say
"aurora borealis," he discovered a
gigantic igloo.

Ralph shook the snow off his muffler. "I'm an explorer," he said.

"Me too," said the bear.

Ralph picked the ice balls off his woolly mittens. "I'm going to the North Pole," he said.

"Me too," said the bear.

Ralph took off his mukluks and wiggled his toes. "It's the one thing I've never done before," he said.

"Me too," said the bear.

They soon became friends. Ralph let the bear try on his mukluks. The bear gave Ralph his favorite globe.

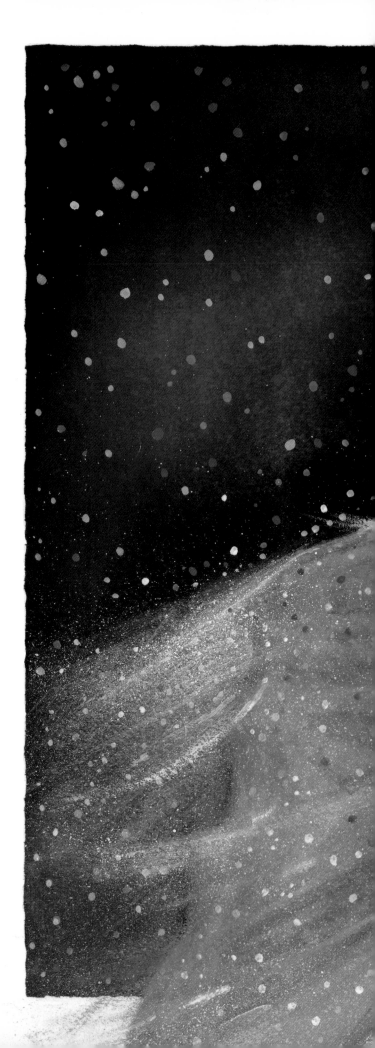

Since they were going to the same place, Ralph and the bear decided to travel together. Although the bear wasn't much of a talker, he was a good traveling companion. For one thing, he had an extraordinary sense of direction and Ralph came to rely on him more and more.

But as they went on, snow fell thicker and faster. The wind picked up and the temperature fell.

"Big storm coming," was all the bear said as he led the way.

Ralph strained his eyes through the swirling white flakes until he felt dizzy. "Holy Cow!" he said. "The only thing harder than trying to see a polar bear in a snowstorm is trying to follow one!

"Bear!" he shouted, but the north wind blew the words right out of his mouth.

Ralph was all alone.

That night Ralph built an igloo just the way the bear had taught him. With the storm raging outside, he sat miserably picking ice balls off his wet woolly mittens and wondering if he would ever get to the North Pole.

Suddenly a tremendous gust of wind thundered out of the north and slammed into his igloo. And before you could say ''musk-ox,'' Ralph was flying through the night.

But while he was whistling
through the air one of his arms
hooked around something.
THUD!

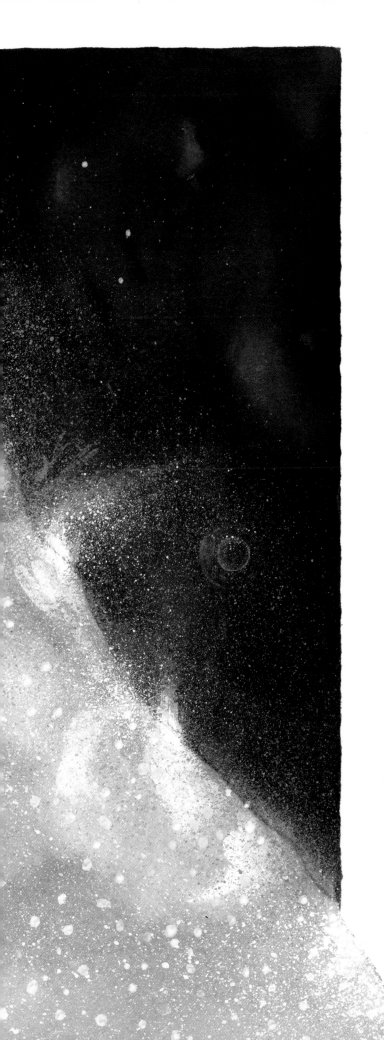

He landed on a lump of snow.

He shook out his muffler. "It's kind of dark up here," he said.

He picked the ice balls off his woolly mittens. "It's kind of gloomy up here," he said.

He wiggled his freezing toes. "It's kind of lonely up here!" he cried out.

"Did I come all this way only to end up sitting all alone on a lump of snow?"

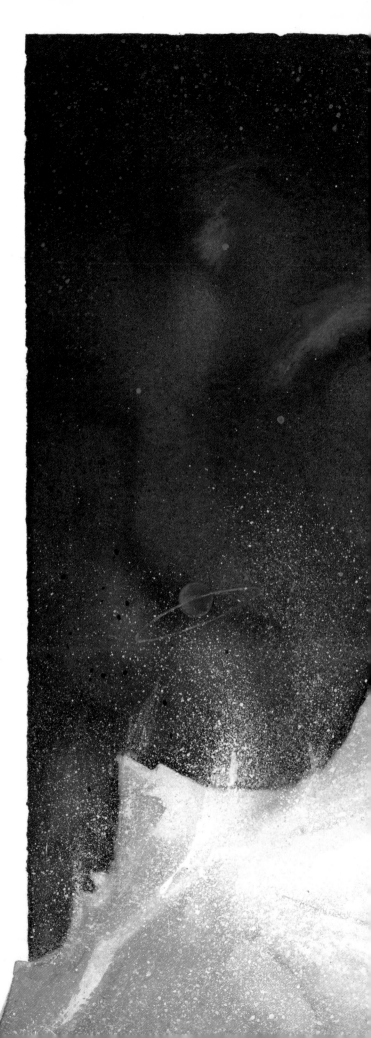

"Nope," a voice said.

Ralph looked down. "Is that you, Bear?"

"Yup," said the bear.

"Are we at the North Pole?"

"Yup," said the bear.

"Holy Cow!" Ralph said. "We've done the one thing we've never done before!"

"Yup," said the bear, "and it's just like I'd pictured it."

"Me too," said Ralph.